Level 2 is 'ideal for children who have received some reading instructio~~n~~ ~~and can read short~~ simple sentences with h~~elp~~

Special features:

Short,
simple
sentences

One day, a nu~~t fell~~
on Chicken Licken.

"Ouch! The sky is falling
down!" said Chicken
Licken. "I must tell
the king."

6

7

Large,
clear type

On the way, they met
Ducky Lucky.

"The sky is falling down,"
said Chicken Licken.
"I'm going to tell the king."

16

17

Careful match
between
story and
pictures

Educational Consultant: Geraldine Taylor
Book Banding Consultant: Kate Ruttle

A catalogue record for this book is available from the British Library

Published by Ladybird Books Ltd
80 Strand, London, WC2R 0RL
A Penguin Company

005
© LADYBIRD BOOKS LTD MMX. This edition MMXIII
Ladybird, Read It Yourself and the Ladybird Logo are registered or
unregistered trademarks of Ladybird Books Limited.

ISBN: 978-0-72327-297-7

Printed in China

Chicken Licken

Illustrated by Richard Johnson

One day, a nut fell
on Chicken Licken.

"Ouch! The sky is falling
down!" said Chicken
Licken. "I must tell
the king."

7

On the way, he met
Henny Penny.

"The sky is falling down,"
said Chicken Licken.
"I'm going to tell the king."

9

"I'll come too,"
said Henny Penny.

And off they went
to find the king.

To the Castle

On the way, they met
Cocky Locky.

"The sky is falling down,"
said Chicken Licken.
"I'm going to tell
the king."

13

"I'll come too,"
said Cocky Locky.

And off they went
to find the king.

14

To the Castle

15

On the way, they met
Ducky Lucky.

"The sky is falling down,"
said Chicken Licken.
"I'm going to tell the king."

17

"I'll come too,"
said Ducky Lucky.

And off they went
to find the king.

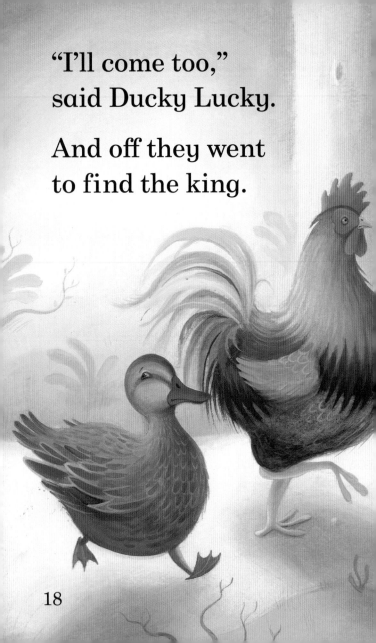

18

To the Castle

19

On the way, they met
Drakey Lakey.

"The sky is falling down,"
said Chicken Licken.
"I'm going to tell the king."

"I'll come too,"
said Drakey Lakey.

And off they went
to find the king.

Farm

To the Castle

23

On the way, they met
Goosey Loosey.

"The sky is falling down,"
said Chicken Licken.
"I'm going to tell the king."

"I'll come too," said
Goosey Loosey.

And off they went
to find the king.

On the way, they met
Foxy Loxy.

"The sky is falling down,"
they said. "We're going
to tell the king."

"The king lives here,"
said Foxy Loxy.
"Follow me."

To the Castle

And that was the end of Chicken Licken, Henny Penny, Cocky Locky, Ducky Lucky, Drakey Lakey and Goosey Loosey!

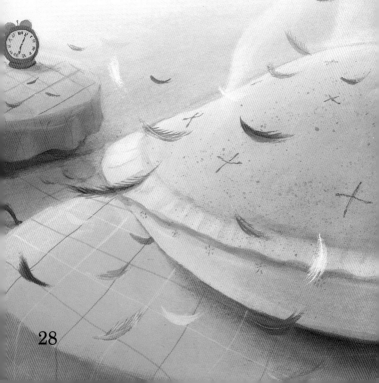

How much do you remember about the story of Chicken Licken? Answer these questions and find out!

- What falls on Chicken Licken's head?

- What does he think is happening?

- Who does Chicken Licken go to tell?

- Where does Foxy Loxy take everyone?